Zoë
Wins the Race

First published in the United Kingdom in 2005
by Chrysalis Children's Books,
an imprint of Chrysalis Books Group plc
The Chrysalis Building
Bramley Road
London W10 6SP
www.chrysalisbooks.co.uk

This book was created for Chrysalis Children's Books by Zuza Books.
Text and illustrations copyright © Zuza Books

BRITISH LIBRARY CATALOGUING-IN-PUBLICATION DATA
A catalogue record for this book is available from the British Library.

ISBN 1 84458 407 0

Printed in China
2 4 6 8 10 9 7 5 3 1

Zoë
Wins the Race

Zuza Vrbova

Illustrated by Tom Morgan-Jones

CHRYSALIS CHILDREN'S BOOKS

Zoë found it hard to make decisions. She took
a long time to decide which books to read.
She took a long time to decide what to play
at playtime.

Her friend Tabby was always saying,
"Come on, Zoë, make up your mind!"

4

One lunchtime, Zoë was very quiet and she didn't want to eat anything.

"Hi, Zoë. What's wrong?" asked Tabby as she sat down next to her.

"Oh, nothing," said Zoë.

"It's not nothing. I can tell," Tabby replied.

"Well, it's sports day soon. I want to do better than I did last year. I want to win a race."

6

"Well, first you have to decide which race to enter,"
said Tabby. "The egg-and-spoon race? The three-legged race?
The sack race? Or do you want to do the hurdles?"

"Yes! I want to WIN the hurdles!" said Zoë.
She was so excited that she dropped her peas.

"Well, you can't leave it to luck," said Tabby. She did a perfect cartwheel as they headed to the playground.

"You are good at everything," Zoë said.

"That's because I practise a lot," explained Tabby.

"I'll help you practise for the race," said Tabby.
"We can start tomorrow. Meet me here.
Same time, same place."

"OK," said Zoë. She was feeling better now
that she had a plan.

The next day, Tabby and Zoë met up in the playground.

"Let's look at the hurdle course," said Tabby.

So they walked across the school playing fields to see the hurdles.

"Here's the start," said Tabby.

They both looked at the first hurdle.

"Can you jump over that?" Tabby asked Zoë.

Zoë wasn't sure. She felt her knees begin to knock. The hurdle looked almost as tall as her.

"Let's count how many hurdles there are,"
suggested Tabby.

There were eight. Zoë wondered if
she could jump over them all.

"I'll never be able to do the hurdle course," said Zoë.

"Yes, you will. Just imagine yourself jumping over the hurdles. Then when it comes to the real race, it will be MUCH easier," said Tabby smiling.

"I think I'll bring my toy rabbit to sports day
to watch," said Zoë.

"That's a great idea. Rupert will bring you luck!"
Tabby laughed.

The next day, on the way to school, Zoë had
a spring in her step.

I'm looking forward to sports day, she thought,
as she jumped over a log.

"Last night, I dreamed I was in the race," she told Tabby. "I jumped over every hurdle perfectly."

"Great!" said Tabby. "It's good to go through something in your mind before you do it."

When they were having lunch, Zoë said, "I think I am ready for the race, but I'm feeling a bit tired from all the practice."

"Well," Tabby replied, "try eating some bananas."

Zoë looked puzzled.

"Bananas will make you full of beans for the race," explained Tabby.

Zoë was even more puzzled. Surely bananas will make me full
of bananas, not beans, she thought. But she didn't say anything.

Tabby then added, "And you better go to bed early tonight."

"Why?" asked Zoë. She thought Tabby was beginning
to sound like her mother.

"Lots of sleep will give you lots of energy," said Tabby.

After lunch, Zoë and Tabby went into the playground.
Zoë's knees began to knock.

"What's the matter?" asked Tabby.

"Well...," Zoë said slowly, "Rudy and Fred are
entering the race and they are much better than me."

"And look at the twins! They are entering too and they are really fast!" wailed Zoë.

"Don't worry about them. Just do your best. Then, even if you don't win, you can be proud of yourself," said Tabby. "Now, let's practise the hurdles again."

And that's what they did all afternoon.

On the day of the race, Zoë turned up looking very smart in her running outfit. The twins were wearing their number-one T-shirts.

Fred was looking very fit and Rudy kept hopping on the spot. There was a buzz of excitement in the air. Even the ground was shaking. (But that was because Harriet was jumping about so much!)

23

Zoë was beginning to look forward to the race until
Tabby asked, "What shoes are you going to wear?"

Zoë sighed and showed her friend her old pair of trainers.

"Why don't you borrow mine?" suggested Tabby,
handing Zoë her own brand-new pair of trainers.

"Thanks. You are a real friend," said Zoë smiling.

Zoë and Tabby had time to watch George and Tommy
pulling each other about in the three-legged race.

Then they watched Misty, Harriet, Fay, Roddy and Leo
in the sack race.

"Come on, Zoë," said Tabby. "Let's go to the start
of the hurdles."

Just before the race was about to start, Zoë was nervous. She looked very pale.

But when the whistle blew, off Zoë went. She flew like the wind, smiling all the way. She could hear Tabby and Miss Roo shouting, "Come on, Zoë, you can do it!" And she saw Rupert waving at her.

When Zoë saw Fred ahead of her, she remembered
Tabby saying, "Just do your best." She sped on.
She didn't notice anything or anyone. She just went
faster and faster.

Suddenly, Zoë felt Tabby giving her a big hug.

Then George pinned a red rosette on her T-shirt.

"What happened?" asked Zoë panting.

"You won!" said Tabby. "That's what happened!"

Zoë was speechless, but she couldn't stop smiling.

Even Roddy was smiling.

"You see, Zoë, you practised hard and then you won!" laughed Tabby.

Top of the Class

Collect them all!

Ellie Takes a Chance
Zuza Vrbova
Illustrated by Tom Morgan-Jones
1-84458-483-6

Zoë Wins the Race
Zuza Vrbova
Illustrated by Tom Morgan-Jones
1-84458-407-0

Piers Finds his Voice
Zuza Vrbova
Illustrated by Tom Morgan-Jones
1-84458-406-2

George Makes Friends
Zuza Vrbova
Illustrated by Tom Morgan-Jones
1-84458-482-8

Tabby Saves the Day
Zuza Vrbova
Illustrated by Tom Morgan-Jones
1-84458-481-X

Kit Paints the Sky
Zuza Vrbova
Illustrated by Tom Morgan-Jones
1-84458-404-6

Leo Takes to the Stage
Zuza Vrbova
Illustrated by Tom Morgan-Jones
1-84458-405-4

Roddy Learns a Lesson
Zuza Vrbova
Illustrated by Tom Morgan-Jones
1-84458-480-1

Visit the Top of the Class website at
www.topoftheclassbooks.com